For Adrian – read if you dare. R.S.

Text copyright © Ruth Symes 1999
Illustrations copyright © Stephen Player 1999

First published in Great Britain in 1999
by Macdonald Young Books
an imprint of Wayland Publishers Ltd
61 Western Road
Hove
East Sussex
BN3 1JD

Find Macdonald Young Books on the internet at
http://www.myb.co.uk

The right of Ruth Symes to be identified as the author
and Stephen Player the illustrator of this Work has been
asserted by them in accordance with the
Copyright, Designs and Patents Act 1988

Designed and Typeset by Don Martin
Printed in Hong Kong by Wing King Tong Co. Ltd.

British Library Cataloguing in Publication Data available

ISBN: 0 7500 2622 7 (pb)

RUTH SYMES

Play...
If you dare

Illustrated by Stephen Player

MACDONALD YOUNG BOOKS

Chapter One

The fog hung around the car boot sale like
an uninvited guest. It kept most customers
away. Not that those who came found much
to spend their money on.

Josie had walked round almost all of the
stalls without finding anything she wanted
to buy. Lucky, really, because she didn't have
much money to spend.

The cold fog seeped into her bones. It was time to go home.

"Hey! You, girl – don't go home yet. You haven't looked at my stall," a voice called.

Josie looked round.

A man beckoned her. He had a straggly grey beard and wore a long black coat. A hat hid most of his face.

The man stood behind a stall Josie hadn't noticed before. She went over.

"Everyone finds what they're looking for at my stall," the man said.

He gave Josie the creeps, but his stall looked interesting. It was selling books and games.

She looked at the books first. Then she ran her fingers over the games. There were some good ones. She tried not to act too interested – in case the man upped the price.

"That's it, that's it, take your time, choose carefully," the man said.

Josie glanced up. The man grinned at her. His mouth was full of rotten, brown, jagged teeth.

She looked down. Her fingers had stopped at a hand-sized rectangular computer game. She'd wanted to buy one of these for ages but they were too expensive.

"It's probably not working," Josie told herself. No one would want to sell it if it were.

She pressed the on button. The silvery screen lit up. Black letters appeared.

Play...
If You Dare

So it *was* working.

The man smiled to himself and nodded his head slowly.

"You'll enjoy playing with that game," he said. "I've never had any complaints about it."

Josie pressed the off button. She didn't want to waste the batteries.

"How much?" she asked.

"Let me see," the man said. He pulled at his beard thoughtfully, "Shall we say five pounds?"

Josie quickly felt in her pocket. She brought out all the money she had. It wasn't enough.

"I've only got four pounds," she said,
"would you put the game to one side for me?
I'll run home and get the rest of the money."

The man shook his head.

Josie had to have the game.

"Please. I'll be really quick. I promise.
I live just across the park."

"Well, that game's meant for you," the man told her. "Tell you what, I'll take what you've got."

"Thanks," Josie said, surprised. She handed over her money and picked up the game. She couldn't believe she'd got something so good for only four pounds.

The game was worth loads more than that.

She started to walk away.

"Wait!" the man called after her.

Josie stopped. She hoped he hadn't changed his mind.

"You'd better take the box it belongs in," he said. He handed her a blood-red plastic box. It had a screaming face engraved on the front.

The box was so horrible Josie didn't even want to touch it. But she had to take it.

She put the game inside the box.

"Have fun," the man said. He smiled an evil smile.

Josie turned and ran as fast as she could across the park.

When she reached the gate she looked back. She could see most of the car boot stalls, but not the one where she'd bought the game.

A thick, white fog covered the place where it had been.

Chapter Two

Josie's parents were in the kitchen making lunch when she got home.

Josie ran up the stairs and went into her room. The walls were covered with posters from her favourite film, *Aliens Save the Earth*. Models of alien spaceships hung from the ceiling. There was even a life-sized cardboard cut-out of Zargon, the alien warrior queen, standing by the window.

Josie threw her coat over a chair. Then stretched out on her bed.

She took the game out of its revolting box and dropped the box on to the floor.

She pressed the on button.

The game's silvery screen lit up and the words *"Play... If You Dare"* appeared.

Josie pressed the button again.

"Are you sure that you want to play?"

"Of course I want to," Josie muttered.
Why else would she have bought the game
from the creepy man?

"Press up for yes and down for no."
Josie pressed the up key pad.
"Name?"

Outside, over in the park, Josie heard a voice shouting, "Don't do it! don't do it!" Some kids must be playing.

She used the direction buttons to spell *"Jo"* for Josie.

The words *"Ready, Challenger Jo? Then let's begin"* flashed on to the screen.

The next moment a complicated colourful maze, with obstacles like trees, bridges and tunnels appeared.

"This looks good," Josie thought.

A tiny figure of a boy ran on to the screen. Josie watched him trying to find somewhere to hide.

The animation for her new game was excellent. All the other games she'd seen had figures that looked more like robots than people.

But in "Play… If You Dare" the figure looked just like a real boy running. Running for his life.

Three masked men ran on to the screen.
Josie was glad that they weren't chasing her.

In the distance she heard one of the
children in the park shouting,
"Help! Help!"

She wasn't sure how she was supposed to play the game. There weren't any instructions.

She pressed a red button and a tree fell over, blocking the path of the three chasing men. They tried to move the tree but it was too heavy. One of the hunters kicked at the tree in fury.

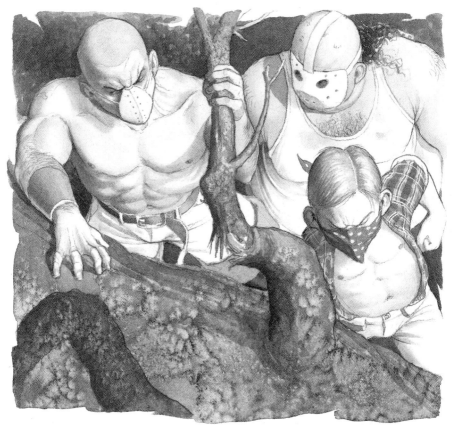

The boy ran off the screen. *"Well done, Challenger Jo. You have stopped the hunters – for now. Are you ready to play level 2?"*

"So the three men are hunting the boy," Josie said to herself. "And I'm supposed to help him get away."

She wanted to play level 2.

"Josie," Mum called up the stairs, "dinner's ready."

"Down in a minute," Josie shouted back. She switched off the game.

Mum came into Josie's room. She frowned at Zargon. "Nasty, ugly thing," she said.

"Zargon isn't ugly," Josie told her mum. "She's a hero."

"Hmm," Mum said, doubtfully, "she'd give me nightmares if she were in my room. Come and have your dinner."

Chapter Three

After dinner Mum and Dad went to dig over
the vegetable patch. They wanted Josie to
help too, but she said she had to do her
homework. She *did* have some homework,

but the real reason she wanted to stay
indoors was so she could play the game.
It was all she could think about.

As soon as Mum and Dad had gone
outside Josie raced upstairs and picked it up.

She pressed the on button.

"Play… If You Dare."

The children were still playing in the park. Josie heard one of them shouting, "Don't do it! They'll get you next."

"Level 2" flashed on to the screen.

This time even more obstacles appeared.

The boy soon came running. It was amazing how life-like he was. The game designer had even managed to make him look terrified.

"Help! help!" one of the children in the park shouted.

This time there were four hunters chasing
the boy. Josie had seen three of them in the
level 1 game but the fourth hunter was new.
He wore a mask that covered his face
completely.

Josie pressed the red button and toppled
a tree over to block their path. This time the
tree stopped only two of them. The other
hunters raced onwards. They were closing in
on the boy.

"The bridge, the bridge," Josie heard
a tiny voice cry.

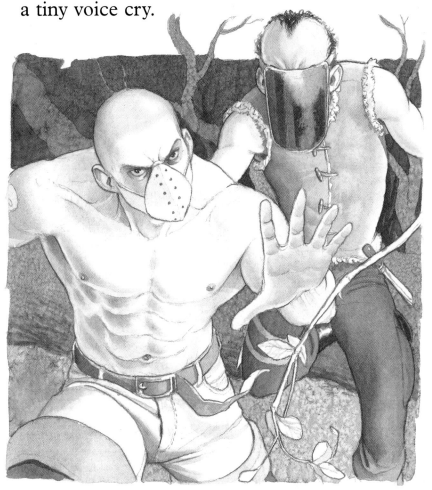

The two hunters were just running over a bridge. What would happen if…

Josie pressed the red button and the bridge collapsed. The two hunters tumbled into the rushing water below.

"That's stopped you," Josie said.

She was very pleased with her skilful playing.

Four alligators swam towards the hunters.

"Urgh!" Josie said, as she watched the
alligators start feeding. It was really gruesome.
Blood and gore crept up the screen.

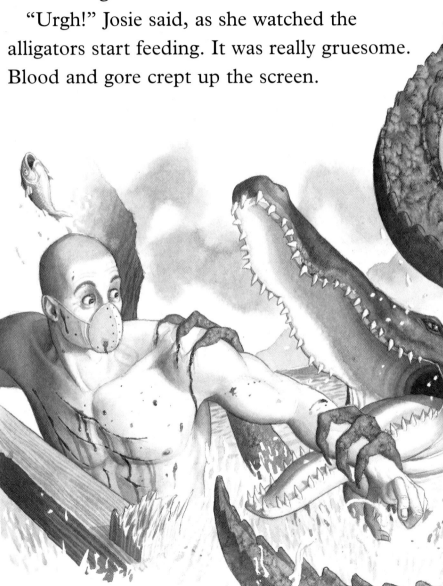

Josie felt a tiny bit sick. The game designer had been just too realistic. The children in the park were playing a noisy game. She could hear them screaming.

Chapter Four

"Good work, Challenger Josie."

Josie frowned. She didn't think she'd keyed in her whole name. She thought she'd only put in the first two letters.

"Level 3. Play… If You Dare."

The game was too good to stop now.

"Stop, please stop!" a tiny voice shouted and just for a moment Josie thought the voice wasn't coming from the park. It sounded like it was coming from somewhere much closer. Inside her room.

Josie pressed the play button.

Once again the boy raced on to the screen, but this time he stopped, turned to face her and cupped his hands around his mouth.

"Don't play!" he shouted in a tiny squeaky voice. "Turn the game off! Now!"

Josie almost dropped the game in surprise. Then she smiled.

How clever!

She didn't know figures in games could speak. She'd have expected it to tell her to play, not to stop playing.

The boy looked behind him then raced for the nearest bridge.

"Too late now!" he cried.

Two hunters came running on to the screen.

This time they brought a slavering, ferocious dog with them. It was straining at its chain lead. One of the hunters unclipped it.

"Do something!" the boy screamed as the dog tore towards him.

Josie pressed the red button and brought a tree down. It missed the charging dog.

The boy ran into a tunnel and the dog ran after him.

Josie could hardly bear to watch.

The dog was so close that at any moment its massive jaws would crush the boy. He would be torn to shreds. She had to do something.

Josie positioned her finger ready. As soon as the boy came out of the tunnel she pressed the red button.

The tunnel caved in.

"Yes!" Josie shouted.

It had been a close thing. But she'd managed to save the boy. Without her skilful playing he'd have been dog food.

Chapter Five

"Congratulations, Challenger Josie. Now it's your turn to play the real game."

'The real game?' Josie thought. Hadn't she been playing the real game?

"Turn it off!" the boy's voice cried. "Quick, before it traps you inside it like it trapped me!"

"Huh?" Josie said.

She pressed the off button, but nothing happened. She pressed it again. She started to feel scared. Very scared. She turned the game over and flicked open the back flap.

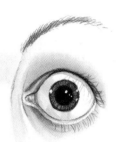

No batteries!

"Your turn now, Challenger Josie."

"Put it in the box!" the boy shouted.

Josie tried to put the game back into its red box. But the lid wouldn't open.

The screaming face on the box started to smile. No, not smile – leer. As one eye slowly winked at her.

Josie screamed.

"Time to change places, Challenger Josie," the screen read.

Josie's hands were starting to fade. She could feel herself draining away.

"No!" she cried.

She had to do something – fast! She looked at Zargon. The alien queen would know what to do... And suddenly Josie knew!

"Take Zargon instead. She's a much better player than me," she told the game screen.

"Zargon?"

Feeling as heavy as lead, Josie dragged herself off the bed and positioned the game so it could see Zargon. She didn't go too close, in case it saw that Zargon was only a cardboard cut-out.

"Zargon will be a worthy game player.
Come, Challenger Zargon.
Play... If You Dare."
Zargon disappeared.

The hunted boy was ejected from the game and fell, life-sized – THUD! – into Josie's room.

He scuttled into a corner and stared in terror at the game.

Josie couldn't move. She felt sick with fear. Her heart thumped loudly as she waited for the game to realize it had been tricked.

It happened almost immediately. Smoke began to fume out of the game. It made strange hissing sounds.

"Error! Error!" the screen read.

"Player not human!

Shut down! Shut down!

Shu..."

The game melted in on itself until there was nothing left but a crumpled ball. Then, with a last hiss, it disappeared. The red plastic box dissolved into blood-red gloop and then was gone too.

Josie stared at the place where it had been.

"It's over!" the boy whispered. "The game's finally over and you..." he looked up at Josie. "You won."

DARE TO BE SCARED!

Are you brave enough to try more titles in the Tremors series? They're guaranteed to chill your spine...

The Ghosts of Golfhawk School by Tessa Potter
Martin and Dan love frightening the younger children at school with scary ghost stories. But then Kirsty arrives. Kirsty claims that she can actually see ghosts – and she sees them in so many places that everyone becomes petrified. Then a mysterious virus sweeps through the school. Martin is still sure she is lying. After all, ghosts don't exist – do they?

The Claygate Hound by Jan Dean
On the school camp to Claygate, Billy is determined to scare everyone with his terrifying stories of the Claygate Hound, a vicious ghost dog said to lurk nearby. Ryan and Zeb ignore his warnings and explore the woods, where they find an old ruin covered in ivy. They hear a ghostly howl – and run. Has Billy been speaking the truth, or is there a more terrifying reason for what they have heard?

The Curse of the Ghost Horse by Anthony Masters
Only Jake believes the eerie tale of Black Bess, a handsome black mare that fell to her death when she was forced to jump a huge crevasse. From that day, bad luck and Black Bess's ghost have haunted the area. Tormented by his father's illness, Jake is determined to jump the crevasse and find Black Bess. But will Jake's obsession lead to his death?

All these books and many more can be purchased from your local bookseller. For more information about Tremors, write to: The Sales Department, Macdonald Young Books, 61 Western Road, Hove, East Sussex BN3 1JD.